Born in ⌐ ⌐ Eastern Canada, the ⌐anada, where she met her ⌐ ⌐ 1978, they moved outside Cambr⌐ ⌐ she taught languages at a private sch⌐ ⌐efore becoming Head of Department. She also organised student trips to Russia, Egypt, Turkey, Germany, New York, Washington D.C. and Kenya and travelled all over the world in the holidays.

Ute Maria has written short stories, novels, plays and also for children. Now she runs a book club at her local primary school where Max and Milky continue their adventures.

Milky and Max
Sail to Saturn

Ute Maria Sproulle

Milky and Max Sail to Saturn

Nightingale Books

NIGHTINGALE PAPERBACK

A CIP catalogue record for this title is
available from the British Library.
ISBN 9781838750169

*Nightingale Books is an imprint of
Pegasus Elliot MacKenzie Publishers Ltd.*
www.pegasuspublishers.com

First Published in 2020

**Nightingale Books
Sheraton House Castle Park
Cambridge England**

Printed & Bound in Great Britain

Dedication

To all aspiring scientists and space travellers.

Acknowledgements

To Jessamy, Sammi-Jo and Richard who have read and approved.

Chapter 1 - Introducing Pella

Another boring day at school. Saint Matilda's School for Girls was such a dump: the dorms were like a prison, the food was gross and the teachers were - well, boring. No other word for it.

Why did my parents send me here? Being scientists, they were always researching, travelling and doing even more research. When they weren't disappearing - as they had before Max and I went to Mars. But you know all about that: how Max's great-uncle, Professor Boggle, got us there so Max could visit his Martian friends. And, of course, my evil aunt Anna - but the less said about her, the better.

Pella was the one good thing about this place. She was my best friend because we shared a bond: we were both named after stars. In my case, I was named after the Milky Way; in her case, Capella in Orion's Belt. I didn't know much else about her but that was enough. Except that she had red hair, which I didn't mind. Mine was, what my Dad called "mousey-brown", which I did mind.

She also had the cutest little dog - curly hair, deep brown eyes that looked right through you and the sweetest smile! Of course, we weren't allowed pets at

Saint Matilda's but Pella had ways of hiding Alpha that were downright devious.

One day I asked, "What does your father do?" after telling her mine was an astro-physicist. We'd already established that our mothers were biologists so fathers were next.

"Oh, I don't see my father much," Pella said, avoiding my - OK, I'll admit it - searching gaze. "He left my Mum when I was two." There was a pause and a shrug. "But he's head of a psychiatric hospital."

"Which one?" I asked quickly. I sensed I knew the answer already.

"The Institute for the Unwell. On the other side of town."

"OMG," I gasped and Pella - not surprisingly - looked as if I was ready to become a potential patient.

"It's where... oh, never mind. There's the bell. Time for class." And I rushed out.

Now, I'm sure I don't have to tell you about Max and how he got just a bit cocky when we returned from Mars. He corrected his science teacher - which you should never do - concerning a fact about space and then Max told him he'd actually been there - to Mars!

Well, that was it - they locked him up! Thankfully, they let him keep Humphrey, Professor Boggle's talking cat, but his parents - as you can imagine - were devastated. And the place they were keeping him in was Pella's Dad's Institute on the other side of town!

I knew what I had to do: I had to spring him. Professor Boggle - or the Martians - would have done it by now, if they'd been able. But the Professor was off travelling with our alien friends and there was no way to get word to him. So, it was now or never - and up to me.

I was imagining Max in that awful place, lounging, lingering, languishing - we were doing alliterations in English - and I had to rescue him, I just had to. Pella was the one person who could help but could I trust her?

At supper that evening I threw a bread roll at a girl who was really getting on my case. She was a bit of a bully anyway, so she had it coming. Unfortunately, the roll bounced off her head and hit a passing teacher. "Who did that? Who is responsible for this atrocious behaviour?"

Bully Bekkie, smirking, pointed at me but Pella jumped in. "No, it wasn't Milky - it was me." She looked contrite but gave me a wink. We were both punished, of course - extra lines - but from then on, I knew I could trust her.

So, all was revealed, even to Humphrey, the talking cat. "Cool," was Pella's reaction.

She agreed to help with my plan. We would call on her father and research the layout. We'd need to disable the alarm system, unlock the doors and then I could rescue Max. A wig and a school uniform for him and mice for Humphrey - that should do the trick.

13

Wednesday was half-day holiday; we were supposed to be studying but Pella got permission to visit her father. I just snuck out.

We headed for the Institute, dressed in our school uniforms, carrying a bag with another uniform we'd "borrowed" - and some dead mice. Dead mice are pretty disgusting but we had a plan.

The guard looked at us suspiciously but when Pella insisted that her father, the Director, would want to see his daughter, he let us in.

The place was spooky, super clean, long straight corridors. Each room had a window - with bars; each door had a window - with bars. Guards and cameras everywhere.

We were taken to the Director's office. Pella's father didn't seem delighted to see her, and even less delighted to see me. Pella put on her best "so-pleased-to-see-you-Daddy-dear" manner. She kept nattering on about school, hobbies, how much she was missing him; asking questions, too.

I got up, "to stretch my legs" - and have a look round, especially at the computers. There were lots of them, monitoring every room, every patient.

Then I spotted him: Max, lounging on his bed, looking dejected, Humphrey curled at his feet. I tried to contain my excitement, my nervousness.

Turning back to the Director and smiling broadly - which made him look at me even more suspiciously - I said how nice it was to meet him and to Pella that we should really be going.

We went. I had memorised the room number and location. We kept smiling sweetly at the guard as we passed and said the Director had given us permission to visit one of the "residents" for "research purposes". He gave a bored shrug, unlocked Number 13 and we entered.

Humphrey was the first to react. Head up, sniffing the air, he yelped, "Mice! They've brought mice!"

Pella reached into her bag, handed him a particularly revolting specimen. Humphrey was in seventh, eighth, ninth heaven!

Max rose slowly, still half asleep, looking whoozy. "Who... who? Milky!" He sat bolt upright, couldn't believe his eyes. He also looked ready to hug me so I got down to business fast.

"Here, Max, put on this uniform and wig. No questions. We're busting you out!" I whispered.

Pella had blocked the surveillance camera with a device Professor Boggle had given us. We'd been able to see him the previous weekend - he always got back in touch on his return - and explain our plans. The Professor approved, told us a few tricks, said he would monitor our progress on his laptop.

Max wasn't quite with it and had to be persuaded to put on a dress and a wig. "We - are - taking - you - away," I emphasised as if speaking to a zombie, which he did resemble. He obeyed.

Now it was Humphrey's turn to play his part. "This is what we need you to do," I explained, bending down. I held another mouse in front of him. "You run out into the corridor with the mouse, past the receptionist - she's bound to be afraid of mice. With any luck, she'll scream and distract the guards."

The cat nodded, clamped on to the mouse. "Don't eat it!" I warned. "Yet."

Pella had taped over the door lock on the way in so we could leave again without problems. The guard was at the other end of the corridor, his back to us.

Humphrey raced in the opposite direction, mouse dangling. Pella and I exited, Max between us. We passed the receptionist, predictably screaming at Humphrey who was demonstrating his skill with mice. She kept calling for the guards who, mysteriously, couldn't receive any of her messages. We obviously didn't tell her that Professor Boggle was jamming the signals.

Max and I walked calmly, as calmly as possible, out the front door, followed by Pella. No one came after us - they were too busy chasing a disappearing cat.

Suddenly Humphrey appeared beside us and jumped into the waiting car. At the wheel sat Professor Boggle, beckoning us in.

"Where are we?" asked Max, still in zombie mode.

Professor Boggle smiled reassuringly. "It's alright, Max. You're safe now. We'll get you home."

"Not his parent's home!" I insisted. "They'll be sure to send him back here."

"No, my home," replied the Professor. "We'll make him well again."

We drove slowly and carefully so as not to attract attention. Once we'd reached the Professor's house, Humphrey jumped out, raced twice around the garden to celebrate his freedom, then into the garage to hunt live mice.

Chapter 2 - An Unwelcome Visitor

The next day explanations were in order. Pella and I obviously had to return to school - we didn't want to arouse suspicion - and the teachers, as usual, were very suspicious.

But it was easy to convince them that Pella's father had been so glad to see her - and naturally me, her best friend - that he wanted us to spend the weekend at his house.

My friend had taken the precaution of sneaking some of her father's stationery. She was very good at forging his handwriting - messy and scrappy - and, what do you know, we got away with it! Luckily her father didn't connect the dots: appearance of daughter and friend and disappearance of inmate. Or so I thought.

We left school Friday afternoon, said we'd take the bus. Real destination: Professor Boggle's house. We had to take Alpha, of course. She was getting tired of being left behind and sometimes barked at the most awkward moments. Either Pella or I would have to pretend that we had had a coughing fit to cover up.

Max was glad to see us and very grateful that we'd sprung him from that cesspit of a hospital.

The Professor explained that Max would be back to his old self in a day or two. I wasn't sure whether that would be an improvement. But I had to admit to being glad that my fellow Mars-traveller was safe at last. How wrong I was.

We relived our trip to the red planet, wondered about our Martian friends, what they were up to. Pella was extremely interested and asked a lot of questions. She seemed really keen to come along on the next mission.

"We're going to Saturn," growled Humphrey as he sauntered in. He and the Professor had obviously been talking. He growled even more when he saw my friend's dog. Alpha tried smiling. It didn't help.

"So," reflected Pella, "it's Saturn then."

I admired her cool. So did the Professor. He asked her what she knew about Saturn.

Pella told him and man, she knew a lot! "Well, the Cassini probe has just finished its mission and crashed into Saturn. Do you realise," and she snuggled down into the sofa, "that it flew through the gaps in Saturn's rings - some of which are ten metres thick in places and some are as thin as tissue paper?"

She looked round as if we were supposed to know this. We nodded, she continued. "The Cassini probe was launched in 1997 and it took seven years to reach Saturn." I glanced at the Professor, who, I assumed, was already working out a faster propulsion system.

"Saturn orbits the Sun more than a billion kilometres from Earth and it's got so many moons." There was no stopping her.

"Eighty-two moons," Max chimed in. He was a bit of a know-it-all so I was glad to see he hadn't changed.

"Did you know that Titan, Saturn's largest moon, has a dense atmosphere and lakes and rivers of liquid methane and ethane?"

Pella was looking pleased with herself which - OK I'll admit it - was becoming faintly annoying.

"Titan is the second biggest moon in the solar system," Max contributed. He wasn't going to give up either. "After Jupiter's moon, Ganymede."

"And Enceladus!" my friend was saying. "Well, that moon has plumes of water spraying from the South Pole and more than 100 geysers."

I was finding this fascinating but really fancied a brownie

No stopping Pella. "I think Europa is my favourite, though. It's one of Jupiter's moons." Weren't we getting off the space track here? "It's icy and –" she paused for dramatic effect, "that would indicate primitive microbial life."

Humphrey's head jerked up. "Mice?" he asked, hopefully. Pella shook her head. "No sorry, Humphrey. Only extremophiles."

I wasn't even going down that road and gave Max a look which stated quite clearly, "Do - not - ask."

"How about lunch," suggested the Professor, not before time.

We proceeded into the kitchen. Lunch was OK, better than mice or extremophiles. But we still had a problem: how to hide Max. Especially when the Professor got a phone call from Max's mother saying she'd been informed by the "hospital" that her son was missing.

The Professor tried to calm her down, said he would investigate and that he'd come to see her soon. Then he returned, looking serious. "That was Max's mother and she's very worried."

"We can't send him back!" I began but the Professor held up his hand.

"No, no, we can't do that. They might experiment on him."

"What do you mean, 'experiment'," I started again but he turned to Pella.

"What do you know about your father's hospital?"

She shook her head. "Not much. It's called 'The Institute for the Unwell' and I've noticed all sorts of people there. Mostly adults, though. Scientists, I think."

Professor Boggle looked thoughtful. "Yes, a good friend of mine was - kept there." He paused. "He never came out."

I was getting a shiver down my spine. "Do you mean he's…" I couldn't say it.

The Professor nodded and bent down to stroke Humphrey. "You knew him, too, didn't you Humphrey?"

The cat, usually so chatty, gulped once and ran outside. Alpha followed despite Humphrey's best efforts to throw her off.

None of us felt like talking much but then Pella asked, "Have you got a way of getting to Saturn, Professor?"

He looked up suddenly as if he'd been dozing. "Well, it is going to be difficult. We've got so many options. There's the slingshot effect from Venus and Jupiter, if the planets are in the correct alignment. Mining an asteroid might be a possibility: breaking down the hydrogen and oxygen atoms."

"Hydrogen we use as fuel," Max added.

"But how do we split the atoms?" asked Pella, still on the case.

This was doing my head in but the Professor was looking more than usually professor-like. "Our biggest problem, of course, is getting out of Earth's gravity and into outer space."

"Once there we could keep on going," pitched in Max again before Pella could. "There'd be nothing holding us back."

I finally chimed in. "Can't we use the Solar Breeze again? Ionised plasma gas and a photon sail?" I explained smugly to Pella. "It got us to Mars."

"Gone. Destroyed." Humphrey had wandered in again, on the lookout for chocolate brownies which he likes even better than mice. Alpha was nowhere to be seen.

"What about anti-matter?" he suggested.

Now a cat with a knowledge of physics is hard to believe, I know. But Humphrey was incredibly smart, having learnt a lot from the Professor.

"Anti-matter?" asked Max, still a bit groggy. "What's that?"

"The opposite of matter," replied Pella, "the shadow of matter." Quite poetic, I thought. "If protons and anti-protons meet, they blow up in a burst of energy."

"That, Pella - and Humphrey - is a very good idea." The Professor was nodding now, looking more and more excited. "If we can siphon off enough anti-protons from a particle beam..." He was off boggling again, dozing into his ideas.

"And the explosion from protons and anti-protons could propel a spaceship close to the speed of light!" Pella was getting excited as well. She saw Max and I looking at her quizzically. "Couldn't it?" she queried.

Again the Professor nodded and smiled. "It's possible, it is just possible."

I hadn't realised that my friend was so intelligent. I was proud of her, of course, but beginning to feel sorry for Max who wasn't getting a look-in.

Suddenly, a sharp rat-a-tat-tat on the front door interrupted us. Humphrey's head jerked up, sniffing the air.

A thin, wiry man with an unusually fat nose stood outside. He was dressed in a neat, dark suit and smiled the sort of smile that gives me the creeps. "Yes?" asked the Professor politely.

"Professor Boggle! Don't you remember me? Your old friend from university? Surely you haven't forgotten Doctor Eustacius Hinklebottom?"

I'd been listening and started to laugh. I mean, who is named Eustacius Hinklebottom?

Pella shushed me. She, too, was listening intently. Max looked puzzled and confused - and slightly alarmed. But that was nothing new.

The Professor also seemed a bit rattled but replied how nice it was to see Dr Hinklebottom and yes, it had been a long time and he had - changed.

"Ah well, we all do. But you, my friend, have not changed at all. Still the same Professor Boggle." Again that smile, the sort that makes you suspicious - and I was.

Professor Boggle invited him in. Dr Eustacius Hinklebottom entered. He was sizing us up, I could tell, especially Max. Pella gave me a look which said, "Do not trust this person." I knew the look, the same one she gives me when we have a particularly nasty teacher.

Max seemed to recognise the "intruder". "You look familiar. Haven't I met you before?"

The wiry man fixed him with a stern, penetrating gaze which made me shiver. "No," he stated before turning back to Professor Boggle. "Tell me about your work, dear Septimus. Any more trips planned?" He seemed to be probing the Professor for information and I think Professor Boggle noticed it, too.

"Oh, nothing much. But you must be very busy, my friend, and we mustn't keep you. Thank you for calling." He ushered the surprised visitor out the door. Humphrey growled, a sure sign that this visit hadn't been welcomed.

Once the Professor returned both Pella and I asked who the big-nosed man was. Professor Boggle shook his head, sideburns bristling. "I'm not sure. He did look similar to my friend from the university. Especially the nose."

"Quite a hooter," Humphrey piped up.

"But I haven't seen him in years and it does seem odd that he should arrive at the very moment that..." He paused and went to sit by Max. "You said he looked familiar. Have you seen him before, Max?"

My space-companion shook his head as if trying to clear it. "I'm not sure but I think I saw someone who looked like him at the hospital. When they were questioning me. But he didn't have such a large nose."

"If you ask me, it looked fake," I volunteered my opinion.

Pella was nodding. "There's a way to find out."
"How?"

"Put a wasp on the nose and see if he reacts."

"What?" I looked round to make sure she didn't have one handy. "How would we do that? Why should he come back here anyway?"

"He'll be back," said my friend confidently.

The Professor nodded again, more serious this time. "I think Pella's right."

Meanwhile, Max was talking to himself, trying to work out ways of getting to Saturn. He was mumbling something about gamma rays emitted from a Black Hole, gravitational waves and neutron stars. He was explaining all this to Humphrey who was backing away cautiously. I worried they might take him back to the Institute.

But Pella was urging me to leave, she didn't want to get into trouble at school. Even though she had a sense of adventure, she was incredibly conscientious and obedient.

We went in search of Alpha who'd been busy digging holes in the garden and depositing you-know-what. You couldn't blame her - she didn't get outdoors a lot at school. We came back to say goodbye.

Professor Boggle was looking thoughtful, his sideburns bushing out. "Yes, you two get back to school. Don't worry, Max and I will sort something out."

Typical - only boys need apply.

Chapter 3 - Another Invention

It was a few weeks before we could visit Professor Boggle and Max again. The teachers were keeping us on a pretty tight leash and Pella was running out of reasons "to visit" her father.

But eventually we managed to sneak out and head over to the Professor's. We knocked but there was no answer. "Garage," I said. It was the most obvious choice.

As not expected, Max - who was looking much better, more alive and not so zombie-like - was working on some sort of - something. Humphrey was keeping watch but didn't growl when he saw us, just said, "Guess who." Then he looked again. "Oh no! They've brought the - thing." He scuttled off. I assumed he wasn't very keen on Alpha, who hid her head in Pella's arms.

"Hi, Milky. Hi, Pella." Max looked absorbed in his twiddling, as only he could.

"What are you working on?" I asked.

"A space elevator," Max replied in a matter-of-fact manner.

"No, seriously."

"Oh yes, seriously. It seems the best way to meet up with our Martian friends."

"A space elevator? An elevator that goes up into - space?" I still couldn't believe it and started to laugh. And once I start, I can't stop.

Max was getting quite cross. "If you'll just let me explain!" he shouted. "It's like this: they've built carbon-nano tubes in the ocean. And a cable has been extended to the space station, which is up there already. The rest of the cable is fixed above that to an asteroid, which acts as a counterweight. It stops the tower or cable flapping about in space. It's 47,000 kilometres long in total."

"Oh, is that all?" asked Pella. She didn't sound convinced either. "So, how would we travel?"

"In between the base platform at sea and the space station we use an electromagnetic vehicle to travel in. We should be able to meet up wth the Martians by the time we reach the asteroid."

Pella nodded and was starting to look impressed. "Well, I have to admit, it does make sense. The problem is," - and her lip curled just a bit - "will it work?"

Max sighed. "Trust me. Or rather, the Professor."

Suddenly I jumped! Pella screamed! Ahead of us was the weirdest creature I had ever seen. One leg, one motor and then another leg was beginning to form. An arm appeared, then another arm. Finally, a circular form which looked like a head and an opening which resembled a mouth.

"Who are you?" asked the creature in a mechanical-sounding voice. "Why are you in Professor Boggle's garage?"

"This is really freaky," I said, trying to show that I wasn't scared, but not making a very good job of it.

"Wh - what is it?" asked Pella, who definitely was afraid.

"Hmmm, well, it could be..." Even Max was struggling to come up with an answer. "Oh, I know - a self-replicating robot."

"What! Are you making this up?"

"No, no. I've read about this." Max was trying to reassure us and not succeeding.

Pella didn't know whether to be impressed or sceptical. I decided that Max must be winding us up. "OK then. Let's go up to it and shake hands with it. Or whatever."

Max didn't think that was such a good idea and the next moment he was proved right.

The arm had just developed a hand which had developed a large fist which started towards us in a threatening manner. "Leave now," it was saying mechanically. "Leave now."

Just then, to our surprise - and relief - the garage door opened.

"Max! Milky! Pella!" Professor Boggle looked both amazed and pleased to see us. "What are you doing here? Oh, I see you've met my Robotron. Don't worry, he's really quite harmless." What part of "harmless" wasn't I getting? "He's just very protective of his space."

As the Professor was speaking, the Robotron was already shrinking, losing his arms, his head, one of his legs until all that was left was the original leg and motor.

"I've designed it on a 3-D printer so that it can perform a particular task - like protecting the house - and then melt itself down and recycle itself."

Max looked slightly ashamed. "Sorry, Professor, I know I shouldn't be in here. But I was hoping to help build something that would get us into space again."

Pella and I looked at each other and decided to keep quiet. We were beginning to feel sorry for Max.

Professor Boggle studied him. "Have you heard from our friends, Max?"

My travelling companion looked away. I knew what he was thinking.

So did the Professor. "Are you worried that our Martian friends have forgotten us?"

Max nodded. There was nothing to be said.

"There may be a lot of reasons why they haven't been in touch," the Professor continued. "There is a lot of space junk floating around up there which could be interfering with transmission signals. And there have been some violent space storms recently. In fact, I'll tune into my pulsar frequency system to see if I can detect anything."

Now I knew that pulsars were the remnants of exploding stars. They generated radio waves which the

Martians would be able to use to signal us. The Professor had once explained it all to us and it had sounded like science-fiction but I could tell that Max was ready to believe anything now.

Suddenly, the Robotron began assembling himself again. What was his problem? Did he still see us as a threat?

Max looked up and turned whiter than the metallic object moving towards the garage door. I spun round and there, blocking the light, was Eustacius Hinklebottom, smiling - not sweetly.

"Well, hello, my dear friends." Since when? "What have we here?" He glanced around at the various gadgets and the magnetic tube Max had been working on. The Robotron kept advancing until Professor Boggle stopped him. "What can I do for you, Doctor Hinklebottom?"

"Oh, just a social call. Hoping I might be able to assist you in your work." He kept his plastic smile pasted on.

I wanted to nudge the Professor and whisper, "Do not trust this person." But Pella had already sprung into action.

Scrabbling around in her jacket pocket, she produced a jar which seemed to be buzzing. "Oh dear, my pet Waspie wants to get out," she called over to me, edging towards Dr Hinklebottom who was studying the magnetic tube. "Whatever shall I do?"

I noticed she was wearing gloves as she unscrewed the lid.

Before I could shout "Stop!", Pella had removed the wasp and placed it on the doctor's nose.

The insect crawled up the huge protrusion and crawled down again. It seemed to be probing or munching or something. Whatever it was doing had no effect on Dr Hinklebottom. He carried on trying to pump the Professor for information on his invention.

Swat! A rolled-up magazine came down on the visitor's "nose". Splat! The "nose" flattened onto his face, squidgy and squashy.

"Oh! So sorry, Dr Hinklebottom. There was a wasp on your nose. Didn't you feel it? My goodness, what is that awful goo all over your face?" Pella tried to look concerned.

"Looks like putty," volunteered Max.

The doctor leapt two feet in the air, fingers on face. Then he ran out the door and down the street. Gone. Alpha was yapping loudly and gave a "do-not-come-back" sort of snarl.

We looked at each other, surprised, confused, laughing. "Well done, Pella," said the Professor, smiling.

"I told you it was fake," said my friend, nodding.

"Hmm," added Max. "He did look like the man at the Institute who kept questioning me about Mars."

"We've got to hurry and finish our space elevator," urged the Professor. "I'll get Robbie to help." So, the creature had a name. That was reassuring.

Pella and I returned to school and let them get on with it. There was only another week left until summer holidays. Soon we'd be back at the Professor's.

Luckily my parents were going on another research trip and happy for me to take part in Professor Boggle's "Science Camp". This was the excuse Max had used when he went to Mars, so it seemed a good way to absent ourselves. Or visit Saturn.

Chapter 4 - Contact at Last

The Professor was strolling up and down in his garage when Pella and I arrived. Max was already there. His parents had been filled in on the need to remove Max and they had agreed to let him go off to "Science Camp" again. Pella said she'd received permission from her mother as well.

She asked how the space elevator was coming on and Max jumped in with, "We've magnetised the plasma in the tube so we should be able to zip up quite quickly."

Was that answering the question? I let it go. Pella didn't. "How did you magnetise it?" she asked.

"Plasma is ionised gas," Max explained patiently, "so it's magnetised already. The carbon-nano tubes are filled with it."

"Yes, bu ..."

"Our spacesuits are equipped with magnets, that's how we slide up," he carried on as if anticipating her question.

"Don't forget the push-pull effect," added the Professor, still strolling.

"Oh yes, that uses dark matter. Which, as you know, makes up 85 per cent of the matter in the universe." Max looked at us to make sure we were following. "And matter exerts gravity which pulls and then, once we're in space, pushes us further."

"Hmmm," was all Pella could think to say.

Max studied us and we must have registered confusion. He continued, "You know that dark matter holds each galaxy in the universe together?"

"Yes, yes," said Pella, sounding annoyed. "And dark energy pushes the universe apart."

Max folded his arms with a satisfied smirk. "As I said, push-pull."

"Wait a minute," I decided to enter the discussion. "This dark energy - is - pushing - the universe - apart?"

"Don't worry, Milky," the Professor tried to reassure me. "It won't happen for awhile yet." So, I could relax then?

As if on cue, a clear beep-beep-beeping sounded from a corner of the garage, followed by a pulsing, throbbing noise. The pulsar radio was transmitting! Finally, the Martians were communicating.

The Professor and Max rushed over. The radio receiver was lighting up, blinking and beeping. They both tuned in to the noise. Pulses and burps emitted before we heard the unmistakable voice of Oog, calling out, "Professor Boggle? Max? Are you there?"

"Yes! Yes!" shouted Max excitedly. "We're both here!"

"We have been trying to make contact with you for so long. Where have you been?"

"Oh dear," replied the Professor. "The receiver hasn't been switched on."

"How are you?" interrupted Max. "How's Zoog? And Moog? And Oogli Woogli?"

"We are all well and prospering. We wanted to ask you: would you like to come with us to Saturn? And Milky, too, of course, if she would like." Would I like? Just try and stop me!

"We need to gather ice from Saturn's rings," Oog continued. "Then we will proceed to Titan and Enceladus for a diplomatic mission."

Max didn't even stop to ask what the diplomatic mission to Saturn's moons was. He just said, still more excitedly, "Yes, please! Definitely, yes!"

The Professor, too, was getting carried away with excitement. "We were just talking about Saturn. My goodness, do you think it would be possible?" He started to explain about his and Max's space elevator.

"Yes, of course, we would need to meet in outer space," continued Oog, "rather than on Earth. It is possible that not all Earth inhabitants are as friendly or as welcoming as you have been to us."

The Professor's sideburns were twitching, always a sign of worry. "I'm still refining our system but it should be ready in a few days and then we'll contact you again."

"We look forward to meeting you." And with one last bleep, Oog signed off.

We looked at each other. So, this was it then.

Or maybe not. The Professor finally admitted that he hadn't quite ironed out all the bugs. Whatever that meant.

Humphrey slunk off when he discovered they weren't real bugs - he'll eat anything! So, it was up to the three of us to help the Professor out.

Pella and I did some research on propulsion systems. What could it hurt if we had some more options?

Max and the Professor went outside to look at the night sky. Mars was low on the horizon and I could hear them reminiscing about our time on the red planet.

I also heard the Professor confess to Max that the magnetised space elevator wasn't "fully operational".

"What do you mean, Uncle Septimus?" When Max was feeling sad, he actually called his great-uncle that, rather than "Professor".

"Well, the magnets aren't properly - magnetised."

"Why not?"

"Not enough power."

Max thought about this for a moment. "We need more magnets?"

"We need more magnets."

"Like a star when it explodes and collapses? And turns into a neutron star with a super-strong magnetic field." Max seemed to be rattling off facts as if he'd been rehearsing them.

I could imagine him smiling proudly but there was a long silence from the Professor. Max must have wondered if he'd said something wrong. I'd crept up to the window by this time so I could listen better - OK, eavesdrop.

"Neutron stars," repeated the Professor, thoughtfully. "Yes, with all that density they could generate a powerful magnetic field, a trillion times more powerful than the Earth's magnetic field."

He fell silent again. I could see Max staring at him anxiously; I was getting anxious myself.

"And," continued the Professor, "there is one coming closer to the Earth's atmosphere in the next few days. My colleague at the university was worried that it might disable one of their satellites."

"Seriously? Neutron stars?" It was out before I could stop myself.

Max, of course, looked annoyed. Nice to know he was back to normal, then.

So now I'll fast forward: neutron stars were out. Too risky. But the breakthrough had come. We were using a space elevator, anchored at one end to a base platform at sea and at the other end (we hoped) to a passing asteroid. That's where we'd meet up with the Martians. In the middle lay the International Space Station - we could dock there, use their solar panels to re-charge and then carry on to the asteroid.

The Professor was going out to the base station to mount the elevator or magnetised tube. (He called it MagTube.) Robotron was helping to assemble the interlinking parts and send them shooting towards the International Space Station. Somehow - don't ask me how - the bottom of the ISS was magnetised enough to receive the MagTube. All we then had to do was re-magnetise the MagTube to the asteroid. Easy.

Luckily Professor Boggle had friends who were helpful and didn't ask too many questions. The whole operation only took a week; the Professor was nothing if not fast. Max helped him, of course. Pella and I had to stay behind, to feed Humphrey - and keep him away from Alpha, not his favourite animal. Oh, and to research Saturn. You know, girl stuff.

Then one day the Professor came back with Max. "We need to leave tomorrow," he announced. Max was nodding, looking incredibly excited.

"But why tomorrow?" asked Pella. She was looking unusually worried.

"A friend of mine is ferrying supplies to the base station. He says - we can come along." For some reason the Professor didn't sound convinced.

"We?" I thought I should check.

"Well, me. But I'm sure it will be possible to smuggle the three of you on board somehow."

Max and I were relieved, of course. Pella looked rather pleased, more so than I would have expected.

Humphrey seemed happy to be left behind. "I'll never understand humans," he grumbled. "Why would you want to go into deep, dark space with all sorts of dangers when you could spend your days sleeping and chasing mice?"

He had a point.

Chapter 5 - Up and Away

We prepared to leave but a problem was developing: Humphrey had changed his mind about staying behind. Once he'd realised that Pella wasn't going to leave her pet dog, he was determined to come, too.

"Alpha has to come. There's no one to leave her with. My Mum will be away, my Dad will - probably experiment on her." I could actually see that happening.

"I'm coming," Humphrey insisted. "You may need me. And," he sniffed, "you definitely won't need - that." He jabbed a paw at poor little Alpha who was looking hurt and confused.

The Professor decided there was nothing else to be done but get more bags.

Two days later we got off the ship at the base of the space elevator and waved goodbye to the captain of the Space Agency ferry. The captain had been surprised to see three children coming aboard but the Professor explained that our parents would be collecting us later in their speed boat, after saying goodbye to him. He believed Professor Boggle - who wouldn't?

So did the commander of the Base Station. He showed us the magnetised elevator - the MagTube, which the Professor had mounted earlier that week - and told us to wait in the waiting area until our parents arrived. He wished the Professor a successful mission to the International Space Station.

"Right," whispered the Professor as soon as the commander had left, "let's get into our magnetised space suits and package you up. And Robbie."

I could tell Max wasn't keen on being packed up with a robot arm and motor - and Humphrey. But he had no choice if he eventually wanted to get to Saturn. Pella was wrapped up snugly and more than delighted to be cuddling Alpha. I was stuffed into a bag.

Soon somebody, or several bodies, were lifting us up, carrying us along and depositing us inside a vibrating contraption. I heard the clunk of a door, then the whirr of what could only be an electro-magnetic engine. We removed our packaging and attached ourselves in our magnetised spacesuits to the magnetised walls of the MagTube. Soon we were whooshing upwards, so fast that it felt like our stomachs had been left behind.

I opened my bag a tiny bit and peeked out. The Professor's sideburns were bushing inside his helmet and there was a big smile on his face. Max, I could tell, was having the time of his life but dutifully not screaming. Pella was the only one who seemed scared, eyes closed, mouth clenched shut. Humphrey and Alpha had been put to sleep to prevent them biting each other's heads off.

Me? Well, I screamed! I was going up in a Space Elevator for goodness sake!

Suddenly there was a screeching sound, a "Boom!" and I felt much lighter, as if I was floating. The Professor had released us into the central hall of the space station.

"My colleague is happy for us to rest here for a few minutes. Yes Milky, he knows about our plans." I wasn't going to ask how or why - best not to. "We need to attach the MagTube to the cable connecting us to the asteroid. That way we'll be able to take advantage of the plasma from the solar flares, and the solar panels on the ISS, to propel us faster up to the asteroid." I figured Max's idea of neutron stars was definitely out. An explosion would probably be too difficult to control anyway. Plus being dangerous.

"Well done, all of you, for helping me with our propulsion problems!" The Professor beamed at each of us and we beamed back. It was nice to be praised and given credit.

"But," he continued, "we've got to wait for our Martian friends to make contact. I'm surprised they haven't already. And my colleague was supposed to meet us here." He looked round and then we spotted him: Eustacius Hinklebottom, minus fake nose.

"Professor Boggle! And friends." Dr Hinklebottom's creepy smile was not reassuring. "I take it you weren't expecting me?"

Well, I wasn't, that was for sure. Neither were Max or the Professor. But, oddly enough, Pella didn't look too surprised. In fact, she had moved over to stand by the evil "doctor".

"I think you know my assistant, Pella?" he was asking us. "She is working for the Director of the Institute and has been most helpful in finding out what you have been up to." Hinklebottom seemed absolutely delighted; Pella wasn't looking at me.

"We're here to visit my colleague," tried the Professor, sideburns bristling. "Where is he?"

"Oh, I would not worry about him. Anymore. I - we - are more interested in that magnetised tube and your connection with Mars." The evil one turned to Max. "I could not obtain much information from this one at the Institute for the Unwell."

Max was looking angrier and angrier and rubbing his wrist and kicking at something behind him. I thought he'd really lost it this time but I was angry myself - with my supposed best friend.

"How could you?" I shouted. "I thought you were my friend. My best friend!"

Pella gave me a strange look, the same look she used to give me when we were planning to play a trick on the teachers. What was going on?

While I was shouting at Pella, Max's footwork had activated the Robotron. I assumed Robbie didn't like being kicked, so he was fighting back. Max stepped aside and pointed at Eustacius Hinklebottom. The robot advanced, fists clenched, determined to cause maximum damage. The evil doctor was taken completely by surprise and pinned to the ground. And sat on, not by Robbie but by Pella!

She squatted on his face while releasing Humphrey and Alpha from their bag. They were both awake, annoyed at having been confined and proceeded to claw at Eustacius Hinklebottom. Max and I helped the Professor to tie up our enemy.

"Robbie can immobilise him," said Professor Boggle with obvious confidence in his Robotron. And, hey presto, the machine managed it! Eustacius Hinklebottom was rolled up tightly and stuffed in a locker labelled "Waste".

"I'm so sorry I deceived you," Pella was saying. "My father - and Dr Hinklebottom - forced me to help him. To find out how you were going to travel to Mars. And beyond."

"But how? Why?" I still felt hurt and upset.

"My father said he wouldn't let me see my mother again. Or let me go back to school. I would have to live with him" - she shuddered - "in that awful Institute."

The Professor patted her shoulder. "You did well to play along. I can't imagine he's found out very much. But I hope he hasn't hurt my friend, the commander of the Space Station."

"I don't think so," Pella answered. "I heard Hinklebottom communicate with my father that he'd keep the commander safe until he needed to return to

Earth. But we've got to hurry or Hinklebottom's crew may arrive before we can meet up with your Martian friends."

"Yes, we must hurry but not before we free the commander." The Professor found his friend and untied him. He explained as little as possible. It was better that way. Then he contacted our Martian friends with the special watch he'd been given by them. The co-ordinates of the asteroid were quickly transmitted, the time of our rendezvous given. (I found out later that "rendezvous" means "meeting up". Cool!)

"Back on the MagTube everyone. Spacesuits on. Follow me." We linked on to the Professor's harness and opened the hatch. Outside the coldness and blackness of space; inside safety, of sorts. Oh well, we were nothing if not adventurous.

We entered the MagTube. Now that we didn't have to hide, we could enjoy the ride. Up, up, up past millions of stars and in the distance was the red planet, Mars, and Jupiter with some of its 79 moons. Further out there would be Saturn with its 82 moons and 23 rings of rocky ice crystals. I couldn't wait!

We looked around for signs of the Martians. Then suddenly there was a hissing sound and it felt as if the MagTube was being sucked toward something we couldn't see. Oh no, it wasn't a Black Hole, was it? Professor Boggle didn't seem worried but then he rarely was.

"Oog? Zoog? Moog?" the Professor programmed his wristwatch. "Is that you?"

"Welcome on board, Professor Boggle. Max. Milky. And friend." Pella was quickly introduced.

Somehow we had been transported onto the Martian spaceship. And there standing in front of us were Oog, Zoog and Moog. Their eyes were bobbling and their arms and legs were jiggling and jangling. So it seemed they were just as pleased to see us again as we were.

Chapter 6 - On the Martian Ship

"This is fantastic!" said Max and Pella in unison. I was so amazed I couldn't do anything but nod my head. We thanked the Martians for taking us along to Saturn.

"It is our pleasure," replied Oog. "We know how much you value our solar system and would like to explore more."

"And we have someone here who wants to re-establish contact," said Moog. Oogli Woogli hugged me and Max and stood back to survey Pella. She reached out a hand and left it up to him to decide which tentacle to extend. The little Martian touched Pella's arm, then bent down to prod Humphrey and Alpha. Cat and dog stood stock still - it wasn't every day they were able to meet an alien.

Caracatus, the Professor's talking computer who had decided to stay with the Martians after we'd been to Mars, rolled forward. "It is nice to see you again, Professor Boggle. And Max. And Milky. And your friend." There was a brief pause, then he added, "I assume you missed me."

It was strange but Caracatus didn't seem to be as grumpy as I remembered him. Pretty sure of himself, of course, but slightly more gentle. Perhaps it was because he had decided to remain behind with Iota, the Martians' translator box. She, too, was saying what a pleasure it was to meet up again.

"How are we going to get to Saturn?" Max couldn't help asking.

"Come with us and we will show you." We all entered the control module, a circular chamber surrounded by windows.

"We will be using the gravitational sling-shot effect to get close to Saturn," explained Zoog.

Max looked puzzled and Zoog, sensing this, explained. "The Earth wants to pull us towards it with its gravity. But we can use gravity to provide us with the push to get further into space. We must just direct our own propulsion system in the right direction."

"Can't we just use your - rocket - all the way there?" I thought I should ask.

"That would take many years to reach Saturn. This way we will use the gravity of all the planets we pass, including your Moon, our own planet Mars and its two moons, Phobos and Deimos, and then Jupiter and its seventy-nine moons." That was a lot of moons. I hoped he wasn't going to ask us to name them all.

"Jupiter will give us a big boost because it is so massive. The bigger the mass, the stronger the gravitational pull." Moog assumed we already knew this. "Therefore, we must be careful not to be pulled towards Jupiter by its gravity but to use our rockets to direct us away. It will then be push-pull all the way to Saturn. In record time."

"What powers your rocket?" asked Pella who had been listening intently.

"Methane, which we collect from Titan, one of Saturn's moons." Moog's googly eyes were fixed on Pella. I wondered why.

Max didn't look like he really understood but he did look impressed. "How quick is 'record time'?" he asked.

"We should be travelling almost at the speed of light which, as you know, is 186,000 miles per second or 300,000 kilometres per second." Either way that had to be impressive - something to write home about. Or not.

The Professor and Max were examining everything and couldn't contain their amazement. They had thought that "gravitational sling-shot effect" as a form of transportation was only possible in science fiction. And now we would be experiencing it for real!

Moog decided that we needed some "nourishment" and took us to what I assumed must be the kitchen quarters. We floated along the corridor and buckled ourselves in. Alpha and Humphrey were left to float about, chasing what might have been Martian sausages. I didn't want to know.

After we had squeezed what tasted like baked beans and broccoli into our mouths and had a drink of "squozen orange juice" - which was squeezed frozen orange juice - we had a nap. Tomorrow - or today - would be another exciting adventure in the vastness of space.

Oogli Woogli shook and rolled us out of our suspended sleeping bags. "Come quickly," he called. "You will not want to miss this!"

We raced to the control module and saw a worried-looking crew. The Professor and the senior Martians weren't very keen to see us. They tried to make us go back but we obviously didn't want to miss out on the fun - or the danger. Although I wasn't too sure about the last bit.

"What's going on?" asked Max, disguising the fact that he was also a little nervous. And worried.

Zoog was calm. "It is nothing of consequence. We are just passing through the Asteroid Belt between Mars and Jupiter. It is throwing up difficulties with navigation."

"Especially one particular asteroid," volunteered the Professor. "It's going in the opposite direction. And seems to have come from outside our solar system." He was looking quite excited about that.

But I was becoming anxious. If you couldn't even trust Martians to navigate the Asteroid Belt - full of rocks and boulders whizzing past every which way - who could you trust? I knew that some of those bruisers could be fifty, even 1,000 kilometres across! I didn't even want to think of the damage they could do to a Martian ship. Or to us!

Suddenly there was a bang and a jolt and a shudder.

"Oh dear," said Caracatus.

"Oh dear," beeped Iota.

Everyone else was silent.

"Are we going to be alright?" I asked, determined not to cry.

"Well…" Zoog began. Then, "We have been hit by an asteroid. Some damage has been caused to our ship. We will need to fix it."

That much was obvious. But who was going to volunteer to go out into outer space and crawl around on a spaceship, trying to find the damage? And avoid being sucked into the next galaxy!

"We have Robbie," suggested Max. "Couldn't he transform himself into a repair kit? And hang onto the spaceship and repair whatever's wrong?"

They all looked at him as if he had just said something brilliant, which he had. "What a wonderful idea, Max!" exclaimed the Professor. He brought the Robotron out of his pack and programmed him.

Soon one arm turned into two, then hands appeared and legs and a body and eyes.

"Robbie, I need you to anchor yourself to the spaceship and find the asteroid impact and fix the hole that it has caused. Your hands will be able to generate a super-glue to fill any gaps. Ready, steady, go!"

The Robotron seemed happy to oblige. We observed him from the window crawling carefully, mechanically along. At one point one of his arms was flapping about and I thought he was going to fly off! But the robot was only making some glue to plug the hole.

Before you could say, "That should fix it!", Robbie was back inside disassembling himself. The Professor thanked him for his efforts, as did the rest of us, but Caracatus grumbled that any intelligent computer could have done that.

I wondered if Caracatus was jealous but I didn't really care. I was just relieved to be safe - and alive.

Since we still had a few million kilometres to go, Moog gathered us children together and took us to another station. Here we were going to have lessons about Saturn because it would be useful to know something about the planet we were visiting.

"How long is a year on Saturn?" she asked.

"Almost 30 Earth years!" Max shouted, eager to show off. "And the outer layer is made of hydrogen. Well, the atmosphere is 94% hydrogen and 6% helium. And it's ten times the distance from the Sun as the Earth is, that's 1,429 million kilometres!"

"Yes, very good, Max," said Moog.

I was also impressed but I wasn't going to say so. What did I know? "It has 82 moons," I said quickly.

"Everyone knows that," replied Max. I stuck my tongue out at him.

"Good, Milky. Anything else? What about you, Oogli?"

"There are 23 rings. They are made of ice and rocks. Some of the rocks are as small as dust particles. Some are large boulders, as large as a house."

"No way!" shouted Max. "You must be exaggerating!"

Oogli Woogli looked puzzled. "I do not know what 'exaggerating' is, but yes way. And the rings are 70,000 kilometres wide and very thin, only one kilometre. They reflect sunshine, so they shine. And there are moons in between the rings," he added.

"Very good, Oogli," said Moog. "And we also need to know that a day on Saturn is 10 Earth hours and 40 minutes long. It is much colder and has very strong winds, about 1,800 kilometres per hour near the equator. So we must be careful there."

Great, I thought, something else to worry about.

Chapter 7 - Almost There

As we floated along the corridor after our lesson, Max asked Oogli Woogli how he knew so much.

Our little Martian friend found it a strange question. "We study and work very hard," he said, "so we can help our civilisation and our planet. And our galaxy. And our universe."

Well, that shut Max up. But not me. "So, can you tell us the difference between weight and mass?" This was a problem that had always puzzled me. "Like why are we weightless in this spaceship and in space?"

"There is no weight in space," replied Oogli Woogli, "therefore you are weightless - because there is no gravity in space, nothing to pull you down. On your Moon your weight would be one sixth that on Earth because your Moon is smaller, less massive and has less gravity."

"Gravity depends on the mass of an object so the bigger the object, the more mass it has, and the more gravitational pull. On the Sun - because it is so massive - your weight would be so great that it would break your legs. If you weighed 25 kilograms on Earth, you would weigh 25 million kilograms on the Sun or 25,000 tons."

"Wow!" exclaimed Max. "That's how much a ferry weighs!"

"Yes, that is if you could stand on the Sun. You would probably fry first."

Well, perhaps we shouldn't go there then.

"What about on Jupiter?" I asked. "How much would I weigh there?"

"Eight tons," replied Oogli Woogli.

"Wow, the weight of our school bus! And on the Moon? You said it would be less than on Earth."

"Yes, you would weigh only 4 kilograms and could jump really high. You would still have your muscles but there would be some weightlessness." Well, that would be really cool.

"The most interesting are comets," continued Oogli Woogli, "because they have very little gravity. If you jumped, you would disappear into space."

Max and I hung on to our straps. It was scary to think what Martians found interesting.

Pella was keeping unusually quiet. In fact, she'd been acting rather strangely, tapping her hand rapidly.

"You alright?" I asked.

"Oh," she turned and looked at me, "it's nothing. Well, not nothing. It's just that I'm wondering about Dr Hinklebottom and what he's up to."

"Surely, we don't have to worry about him, do we? Didn't the Professor stuff him into rubbish disposal?"

She shook her head. "You don't know my father. He's determined to get at the secrets Mars and Saturn hold. And I'm convinced that Dr Hinklebottom had help. Not just me," she added, looking suitably ashamed. Or trying to.

I couldn't help myself. You'd think you should be able to trust your best friend but somehow I was feeling slightly suspicious about Pella. What was her real connection with Dr Hinklebottom, I wondered. Why was she still worried about her father? And where was her mother?

Just then I noticed the Robotron behaving strangely, too. Why would Robbie be assembling himself without Professor Boggle's instructions? A light in his head was beeping and flashing. This made me even more suspicious - and scared.

"He's receiving a signal!" shouted Max. "Someone is programming him!" He was staring at Pella. I could tell he didn't trust her.

My best friend - or so I thought - had a device in her hand which she was using to give Robbie instructions. Was he trying to tie Max and me up? Not if we could help it!

Max used all his Astroball training from his time on Mars to weave in and out. I picked up a Martian directional stick and started hitting the berserk robot - and Pella who'd gone too far this time!

The Professor and the Martians rushed in: they must have been observing our activities on their screens.

"What on Earth - or what in Space?" exclaimed the Professor. He quickly re-programmed Robbie and got him to contain himself back into his case.

Pella - if that was her name - collapsed in a heap, sobbing. I had achieved my aim, being pretty good at field hockey and sports in general.

Max started to explain about the Robotron and Pella and that "it made no sense!"

I chimed in. "She had a controlling device and Robbie was going to attack us! We defended ourselves! Against her!" I pointed angrily at my former friend.

"What I don't understand," added Max, also not happy, "why was Pella programming Robbie?"

Moog's bulging eyes were fixing Pella with a searching, almost sad look. "Her name is not Pella," she said. "It is," she checked her translator device, "Rapella."

"Rapella! Who is named Rapella?"

"She is." Moog pointed at the object of our anger.

"How could you lie to me? Again?" I shouted at the wretched-looking girl. "I thought you were my friend - my best friend!" I'd probably mentioned this before but it was worth repeating.

There was no time for an answer. Suddenly the navigation system beeped that we were approaching Saturn. It was all hands on deck.

Oogli Woogli called down a bubble to keep Pella - or Rapella- "safe". Safe from us, I suspected. I glared at her as I left. She did not look as sorry as I thought she should.

Chapter 8 - Saturn at Last!

As we entered the command module, we could see the outer rings approaching: sparkling, twinkling icily in our directional lights. In the distance were low clouds, resembling a deep, red rose. It was so unbelievably lovely!

"The rings of Saturn!" Professor Boggle was saying. "We're getting close!" I could tell he was just quivering with the excitement of it all. "The Martians are getting ready to harvest some ice which they need as a water source back on their planet. But," he whispered to us, "it is a bit dangerous if we get too close to the rings."

"Why?" asked Max, probably wishing he hadn't.

"The gaps in the rings create warm and cool bands in the atmosphere. Those temperature differences create powerful storms. Up to 1,800 kilometres per hour." I knew that.

Just then Robbie appeared, arm and motor and head and mouth. Where had he come from? And why wasn't he watching Rapella?

"Professor Boggle, it is not wise for Max and Milky to be in here. They should be strapped into their module.

I will take them back there." He was talking now? As if he couldn't get any more obnoxious, another arm was beginning to form. Both arms reached out for Max and me.

If I thought before that I didn't like this computer-robot, now I was sure. Who was he - or it - to tell Max and I what to do? We were here on an adventure and Robbie Robotron could just float on off!

"Thank you, Robbie," said the Professor, "but Max and Milky will stay with us. We do, however, require your services. Could you and Caracatus help the crew collect ice from Saturn's rings, please? You did such an excellent job repairing the spaceship and we need you outside again."

He winked at us and whispered, "It pays to flatter computers - and robots. It makes them feel important. I used to have to do it with Caracatus, too."

We watched as the tubes and containers were released out through the hatch and one computer and one robot skimmed along the rings of ice and dust. They managed to avoid the larger rocks although Caracatus didn't look too happy about it. He was bigger than Robbie and an easy target for any of those boulders the size of a house. The Robotron, on the other hand, could easily retract an arm or a head if something came whizzing towards him.

"Are they going to the inner rings as well?" asked Max, looking a bit worried for Caracatus. I didn't really care what happened to Robbie.

"No," replied Oog, "they must keep to the outer rings, close to us, because there the ice is young and cleaner." He pointed to an instrument panel. "You can see it here on the spectrometer. The cleaner ice is blue, the older, dirtier ice is red."

The light was catching the ice crystals and reflecting back. The shimmering effect was incredibly beautiful and out of this world!

Still, I couldn't stop thinking of how Pella, or Rapella, had tricked us. Then I remembered Alpha! Was she a real dog or - I shuddered - an alien dog?

I went in search of the little creature and couldn't believe it! Humphrey and Alpha were sleeping peacefully together in one of the pods where Moog had placed them. She explained that, yes, Alpha was a real dog and she hadn't been programmed by Rapella to do evil things to the Professor's cat.

Humphrey would have been able to take care of himself but it was a relief to know we had one less thing to worry about.

Moog urged me to return to the command module. I was just in time to hear Iota bleeping furiously. Once the Martians had tuned her in, she said quite clearly, "Caracatus is having difficulties."

They looked and, sure enough, he seemed to be tangled up in one of the tubes! Robbie was trying to help, but not very successfully.

"We will have to go in closer," said Zoog, "and free him."

"It will be dangerous," added Oog, matter-of-factly.

Max and I looked at each other. But we were certain the Martians wouldn't leave Caracatus all on his own out in the dangerous darkness of space.

They were manoeuvring the spaceship closer and closer towards the tubes, trying to pull them in. All of a sudden, a loud whistling sound and a flash of lightning shook the ship.

Moog was the first to say, "A lightning strike! They're called 'whistlers'," she explained to us. Not a comforting fact.

Although "whistlers" sounded interesting - and cute - Max and I weren't in the mood to be interested. We just wanted Caracatus back safely inside, even Robbie, and this ship to stop rocking and shaking so violently.

The next moment our wish came true! Standing in front of us, trembling as much as computers can, was Caracatus. Iota was standing very close as if she didn't want him to go outside a spaceship ever again. Robbie had managed to cling on, while the whistlers were whistling, in order to finish the job. Soon he, too, re-entered and was praised by the Professor and the others.

"Well done, Robbie! Well done, Caracatus! A wonderful achievement!" we all chorussed.

"Could we land on the ice rings?" I asked, ready for another adventure.

"Well, that would be a bit risky," explained the Professor.

"Can't we at least land on Saturn?" Max wasn't going to give up either.

"No, it is the coldest planet in our solar system," replied Zoog. "On the surface, the highest temperature is zero degrees centigrade and the lowest minus 250 degrees centigrade." I was beginning to shiver.

Oog was pointing out the window where a stupendous light show was happening. "It is Saturn's Northern Lights - mainly ultra-violet." I'd never seen anything so beautiful. "Different light particles are being excited and these make a 'whoo' sound," he continued.

Max couldn't help himself. He started making "whoo-whoo" sounds and was floating about, giggling.

"Best to strap yourselves in," advised Moog, who was probably trying to keep Max calm. "Now we will be skating."

Skating? Was I going to get my wish? Wow! Moog was right: the Martian ship dipped, diving and skimming the icy surfaces of the rings, flying between the gaps and sliding over the next. Sadly we couldn't skate all the rings because suddenly...

"Oh dear," said the Professor, looking at the panels. "There seems to be a storm brewing, a big one - 1,250 miles across!"

So, no more sight-seeing then. The 82 moons, the 23 rings, not to mention the thousands of smaller ones with white and orange ice crystals would have to remain unvisited.

"We must head further out," Zoog was saying, "towards Titan. Its winds will help push us."

"Five hundred kilometres per second," Oogli Woogli whispered to us.

"It's just so big!" gasped Max, who couldn't take his eyes off Saturn even as we were speeding away from it.

"Yes," continued Oogli Woogli, "764 of your Earths would fit inside it." That was a lot of Earths. "The surface is very cold but the inside is very hot. The core temperature is 11,700 degrees celsius. You would be toast."

Why, oh why did Oogli Woogli have to keep giving us disturbing facts? All we wanted was to enjoy the view!

Chapter 9 - Touching Titan

Well, there was no time for that. We were plummeting through the purple crown surrounding Titan, Saturn's largest moon, and down, down, down into its yellow-orange mist.

We could see rocks eroded by ice, shaped by flowing methane which looked like a dark, mushy, gloopy ocean. Above that were hills and mountains. Occasionally a volcano of ice spurted up liquid lava from the crust.

There were also gale-force winds which buffeted our spacecraft. I managed to spot huge cloudy tails, "1,000 kilometres in length," the Professor told us.

It was difficult to see where to land. We had learnt that liquid methane made up most of the surface - so, tricky. But since methane ice formed the bedrock and it was minus 200 degrees celsius, perhaps we'd find a hard base?

"I think I see an iceberg down on that ocean!" shouted Max, carried away with the excitement of being on, or near, an alien world. "Can we land there?"

"Too difficult at the moment," replied Oog, steering his ship very carefully. "Saturn's gravity is still too strong. We must go to the other side where Saturn's pull will be less."

That sounded fine, as long as we could get away from the ice pebbles hammering on our heat shields. Or those methane raindrops - "as big as my fist!", Max was shouting at me.

Now don't get me wrong, I liked adventure and exploring. But sailing round an orange ball, which seemed to be inflating and deflating and showering us with rocks, was becoming boring.

Zoog, Oog and Moog were consulting their computers and shaking their tentacles. Radio signals had been exchanged with the Titanics but they didn't seem to be in a welcoming mood.

"We must proceed to Enceladus," Oog explained to us. "The Titanics want us to start our diplomatic mission."

"Could you explain, please, what this 'diplomatic mission' is?" asked the Professor. I was curious, too. Max and Oogli Woogli were counting methane raindrop-bombs.

"We will explain as we travel along," was all I remember hearing before I fell asleep, dangling in my sleeping bag.

Sometime later I woke up in another chamber beside Max and Oogli Woogli, also suspended above a clear surface. Alpha and Humphrey were there, still asleep. Moog must have moved us away from the scene of action.

That was alright by me since we needed to fly, as Oogli Woogli explained, to the outermost icy ring of Saturn. That would probably take ages, I thought, as I tucked into a Martian snack - don't ask - and swayed back and forth.

But I reckoned without Martian know-how and the speed of light.

"Three hundred thousand kilometres per second!" Max was shaking me and going slightly berserk. "We're travelling at the speed of light!"

"Huh? What?" I was trying not to fall out of my sleeping bag and focus at the same time.

"We are tapping into the dark energy which is accelerating at the rate the universe is expanding," explained Oogli Woogli, sensing, once again, confusion.

"Right," I replied. What else could I say? If I wasn't confused before, I was now. And that Martian snack was revolting.

We were definitely travelling fast, that was certain. I felt my insides being pressed together, the snack was threatening to erupt. Before you could say, "Whoosh!", we were facing Enceladus.

The descent was something else - beyond scary. Plumes of icy water were spraying out into space - and at us! It took some pretty nifty navigating by the senior Martians to avoid those monsters.

We were looking down on trenches - "Tiger Stripes" the Professor called them - running through the surface of Enceladus. Ice particles were spewing out of them and falling back like reflective snow.

"These are quite interesting liquid ejections," explained Oog. "They could provide chemical energy if the Enceladians would allow us to harness it."

I thought a minute. "Enceladians? What do they look like?"

Oog checked his translator pad. "Extremophiles. Water bears - eight legs."

"Eight legs?"

"That is correct. If there is no water, they dry into husks. Then they re-hydrate when water falls. They refer to themselves as 'Snottites'."

"Ooohhh, how gross!" I couldn't help myself.

Max looked excited and eager to explore - I knew that look. "Can we land and meet them?"

Zoog, who was steering around the plumes, shook his head. "The surface is minus 200 degrees celsius. These jets of water that we are avoiding are made of ice. They come from a salt ocean under the surface."

"Your suits and our skin are not adapted for these extreme conditions," explained Moog. She could tell Max was disappointed. I wasn't.

"So, how do we communicate with them?" asked the Professor, who also looked a little disappointed.

"Gamma rays," replied Oog.

"You mean, 'distant explosions in space'?"

Oog smiled. "You are well informed, Professor. In seconds they will release more energy than the Sun will put out in its life-time."

"Amazing."

Really? Not scary?

Max just wouldn't give up. "But how do the Snottites survive in those extreme temperatures?"

"They can be frozen for years. But if there is any warm material, such as in their trenches, then they can come alive again within seconds. They can eat and reproduce as if no time had passed. But they need food."

"That is so cool," continued Max. "What do the Snottites eat?"

"Methane gas. As you have discovered, Titan is composed mainly of nitrogen and methane."

"So, the Snottites get their methane from Titan?"

"That is the problem. The Titanics do not want to give their methane to the inhabitants of Enceladus."

"But how did they, these Snottites," - I still found the name gross - "get to Enceladus?"

There was a silence as the Martians looked at each other. "I am afraid," Zoog finally answered, "that your planet sent them here. I believe your space agency wanted to explore the universe and do experiments."

"Oh dear," I said.

"Oh dear," echoed the Professor and Max.

"So, we have contaminated the Universe," added Professor Boggle sadly.

"Possibly," said Oog, " but the Snottites have now been on Enceladus for so long that they are part of this moon. There were no life forms before. And they do not harm the environment. They eat only gases which the Titanics were once happy to provide."

"Were happy?" I asked.

"Yes, now the Titanics think they are superior to the Snottites."

"Why?"

"Because Titan is a larger moon, Saturn's largest, and the second largest in the solar system. Enceladus, as you know, is the smallest."

"But that doesn't seem fair!" Max was getting really upset now. "Just because someone is bigger than you, that doesn't mean they're better!"

I had to agree with that. Max was bigger than me and he wasn't, you know…

"How can we help?" asked the Professor. "Is there a way we can get the Titanics and the Snottites to communicate with each other?"

This time Moog was shaking her head and looking sad. "We have tried. So many times. But the Titanics do not want to send the Snottites any more methane until they agree to become part of their empire."

"Their empire?"

"Yes, they want all the moons to join together to form an empire with Titan as the leader. The Titanics are, what you would call" - she searched her translator pad - "bullies."

Max and I looked at each other. We knew all about bullies.

"But," offered the Professor, "surely we could harness Saturn's gravity to open up Enceladus' Tiger Stripes. Then the plumes would burst forth and the hydro-thermal activity below could produce methane. Which they could eat."

I was beginning to follow this, very slowly. I could tell that Max was, too, by the way he was jumping up and down. "That means they can become independent of the Titanics! They won't be able to bully them anymore!"

"What about Saturn?" I asked. "Will it co-operate?"

"Oh yes. The ice volcanoes on Enceladus replenish Saturn's rings. There are 100 geysers which throw out ice crystals into space and they are trapped by Saturn's rings. Saturn needs Enceladus and, I am sure, would be happy to help."

So, we had a plan then.

Chapter 10 - The Plan Fails - Almost

Well, time just seemed to speed into space what with harnessing Saturn's gravity to release the methane from the tiger stripes. The Snottites were very grateful that we were helping them to become self-sufficient. It was the least we could do.

Max and I were disappointed that we couldn't land and get to know the inhabitants of Enceladus. Communicating with clicks on the Martians' part and slurps from the Snottites just wasn't the same.

Now the Martians were off to Titan to explain about their plan and their methane no longer being needed by the inhabitants of Enceladus. Professor Boggle, Max and I were playing "count the stars and moons" - and missing home.

"How long will it take us to get back?" I asked. I was thinking how much I missed Earth, how beautiful our blue-green planet was.

"Ages," Max said, looking into the vastness of space. I could tell he was missing his parents, too.

"Well, you know our Martian friends," replied the Professor. "They have such an advanced propulsion system, they'll get us home in no time. Or space-time."

The Martians returned. Their tentacles were not waving, their eyes were not bulging. I was guessing things had not gone well.

Professor Boggle asked whether their diplomatic mission had been successful.

"Unfortunately, no," Zoog answered in very monotones. "The Titanics do not like the fact that now the Snottites are independent of them and can produce their own source of food."

"But," Max looked confused, "can't they still be friends?"

"We have all hoped for that," added Oog. "They are both moons, they both depend on Saturn's gravity. They contribute to Saturn's rings. So much in common," he reflected sadly.

I was about to say something really nasty about the Titanics but Moog was speaking. "There is worse news. They are threatening to attack Enceladus. And us."

"Attack?" Max and I screeched. "How do you mean 'attack'?"

"The Titanics have very powerful methane bombs. They can propel them through the gaps in the rings when Enceladus transits Titan," explained Zoog. "And they hide themselves inside these bombs and emerge to attack their victims."

"But - but - can't we just leave?" I wasn't too keen on being anywhere near methane bombs.

"That will be difficult," continued Zoog. "The government of Titan is upset with us for helping the inhabitants of Enceladus. They have refused to give us the methane gas we need for our return trip."

"But," asked Max, still confused, "can't we use the methane from Enceladus? Now that they've got their own source?"

The Professor shook his head. "We must leave them that. We've caused enough damage already. Remember what I once told you: take nothing away and leave nothing behind but footprints."

"Can't we do without it?" It was my turn to ask.

Zoog shook his head. "It is not so easy. Our propulsion system is thermo-acoustic. It depends on the heat of the Sun and the coldness of outer space. The difference between the two - hot and cold - causes vibrations which are converted into the electric energy that powers our ship."

"But," continued Oog, "here, near Saturn, we are too far from the heat of the Sun. So we need methane gas to give us an extra boost."

"Ah," we three humans said, trying to sound intelligent. But I was pretty sure we didn't really understand it all. And we were still in a state of shock. Try to help and where does it get you? But, as the Professor said, "At least we tried to do the right thing."

Suddenly a violent explosion vibrated through the Martian spaceship. Flashes of light penetrated the command module. We were flung in all directions and just managed to cling on to our straps while Oog, Zoog and Moog tried to regain control.

"We must descend to Enceladus," Moog said, "And help them. They are being attacked."

And us, I thought. So, what choice did we have?

Down, down, down through icy rain until we touched harder ground. The Snottites were crawling out to meet us and trying to put a protective slime shield around our ship to protect it from the cold and the methane bombs. They were rather cute: eight legs, pointy little claws, snotty noses - but cute.

"What can we use to attack back?" Max asked. I could tell he was really fired up. He seemed determined to go outside and lob missiles at the Titanics who were surrounding us. We couldn't see them because they were hiding inside their methane bombs, coming at us thick and fast.

The Snottites had sent their representative to meet us under our protective shield. When they heard Max urging us to take up arms and suggesting all sorts of tactics, they must have assumed he was some sort of leader. Why, I had no idea.

"They want Max to be their commander," Oogli Woogli whispered to me. Max? Really? Not me?

Before we could strap him down, Max was outside the shield, in his spacesuit - which really wasn't suitable for being outside. He raised his fists at the Titanics. "You leave my friends alone," he shouted. "You big fat bullies!" We couldn't really see much through all the ice and gas and methane bombs. The Titanics were definitely acting like bullies. I was terrified!

Robbie Robotron was instructed to drag Max back. We could tell it was a mess out there: Titanics throwing methane boulders and the Snottites throwing, well - slime. They were very good at ejecting goo out of all their openings. It was gross, but it worked! The Titanics weren't going anywhere after being covered in gunge and sticking, frozen, to the surface.

Then the whole battle seemed to be over. Max, still very excited, was communicating with the Snottites and the Titanics - Oogli Woogli was translating - and telling them to "Sort it out! Make peace, not war. Max has spoken!"

Okay, he was getting a bit carried away with this leader thing - which was becoming annoying - but he was entitled. He'd brought peace to Enceladus, the Titanics had been put in their place; Max had ruled!

We warmed him up, checked his spacesuit for damage. I could still smell the methane - and the slime.

"You've done well, Max," said the Professor, patting him on the shoulder. "It seems the Titanics have apologised and will not impose their empire on the

Snottites. We've managed to undo some of the harm our species has done." He turned to me.

"And you, Milky, did well to support Max." I suppose I did, by not telling him he was crazy. So, well done me then.

The Titanics, however, didn't want to give us the methane we needed to get home - they were still in a huff. The senior Martians and our Professor Boggle went into a huddle. I could tell he was boggling again, trying to work out a solution.

Max and I looked at each other, shrugged, and went in search of Oogli Woogli. We floated down one of the tubes and noticed our little Martian friend at the far end. He was looking distracted, playing with his iphone-like device. Computer games? Seriously? At a time like this?

"Oogli, what are you doing?" Max finally asked.

Oogli Woogli looked thoughtful. "I have noticed two neutron stars colliding."

"You're kidding! Where?" Max was actually interested. I just thought, great, more bad news.

"In a galaxy far away. One hundred and thirty million years ago. The signals are reaching us now."

Fascinating as this was, I couldn't quite see how colliding neutron stars would help us get home.

"Neutron stars," Max was nodding, as he does. "I was thinking about those. Ordinary stars burn out. And then they turn into dense bodies with really powerful gravity." He looked pleased with himself. Again.

"Yes," agreed our friend, "you are correct. The gravitational field is so powerful that something small falling into it will release as much energy as 1,000 hydrogen bombs."

"Wow!" yelped Max, before asking, "How small?"

"Like," the little Martian checked his translator box, "marshmallows."

I did some quick calculations - I'm good at that - and thought I should contribute. "Well," I said, with some smugness, "I just happen to have a bag of marshmallows."

Yes, I know what you're thinking: how unlikely is that? But I always carry a bag of treats because, trust me, you cannot survive on squashed Martian slugs. And you never know when treats might come in handy - like, apparently now.

So, here was the scene: Martian ship needing energy to return to Mars and us to Earth. Colliding neutron stars, needing a marshmallow to create energy. I had marshmallows.

Now, I wasn't going to ask them to beg, but they would have to ask nicely. At that moment Oogli Woogli and Max were just staring at me, open-mouthed.

The others came to look for us and asked what was going on. Oogli Woogli explained rapidly in clicks and squeaks what he had discovered and what I had said. Max did the same for the Professor, only in English. They were all impressed.

I smiled and handed over the marshmallows. Thanks would not be required. I just hoped this was going to work.

Chapter 11 - Another Plan Succeeds - Just

It was all hands on deck for the next stage. Oog was steering the ship as carefully as he could, as close as he could, towards the neutron stars.

Watching two neutron stars colliding is truly something out of this world - or out of this Universe. Fireworks don't even come close.

Once we were in position, I was allowed the honour of shooting my marshmallow towards the gravitational waves which the collision had created.

Luckily the Martians had the right sort of equipment. Of course, I worried that the marshmallow would turn all squishy and squashy with the pressure. But it seemed to do the trick.

In no time at all a force like two giant hands was pushing us along - fast, really fast. Blazes of light, stars, moons streaked past the windows. We hung on to our suspension straps for all we were worth.

Then the news we had been waiting for: Oog assured us that we were in interstellar space and moving as fast as was possible in interstellar space.

Well, one problem solved. But we were forgetting someone - or something. "What are we going to do with Rapella?" I asked Moog. "And who, or what, is she?"

"Rapella is from a distant planet, in another universe. She has travelled to Mars before and wanted to find out the secrets of our technology. But we banished her when we discovered that her civilisation did not want to use it for peaceful purposes."

"We think," added Zoog, "that is why she agreed to work with the Director of the Institute. Both he and Rapella wanted to know what Max had found out on his trip to Mars. But Saturn was a bigger prize. There are elements on Titan which this Director and Rapella wanted."

"So, she was using this Hinklebottom to help her!" I finally realised. "It all makes sense now. She wanted us to trust her so she had to invent an enemy we could all fight against."

"Yes," agreed Moog, "and when he proved ineffective, she - dumped him. Is that correct?"

"Very correct," I replied, hoping that Hinklebottom was by now at the bottom of "Waste Disposal".

"But what is on Titan that they wanted so badly?" asked Max.

"Titan has a type of plastic which is produced in the active atmosphere of its icy highlands. It is very durable and long-lasting."

"But that is monstrous!" exclaimed the Professor, sideburns twitching and bristling. "As if the Universe didn't have enough plastic rubbish!"

Moog carried on. "It is a natural process. But I suspect this Director and Hinklebottom and Rapella wanted it for a purpose which is not good for your planet or for the Universe."

The Professor was off again. "I'm sure of that! Probably something that has to do with making money!"

The Martians were transmitting confusion. "We do not think that Rapella's civilisation or the Titanics deal with money."

"Power then!" continued the Professor angrily. "If someone wants something badly enough, they will do anything, use any force to get it! So they will be even more powerful!"

I was becoming a bit worried about the Professor; he obviously felt strongly about this. It was how I felt about best friends betraying you and how Max felt about bullies.

We went in search of Rapella because I wanted to give her a piece of my mind - a bad piece.

Moog, Oogli Woogli, Max and I floated along the corridor and entered the chamber where we had left her suspended under a bubble. The bubble was empty.

"She's gone?" Max couldn't believe it. I was speechless.

"She has de-materialised," explained Oogli Woogli, looking around the chamber. "Her particles must be in temporary suspension. Eventually she will need to re-materialise. Otherwise she will disappear."

"Well, I hope she does disappear!" I called out, really angry now. "Forever!"

Meanwhile, Moog was using what looked like a tennis racket to sweep the air.

"Looking for particles of Rapella," Oogli Woogli explained.

Max nodded. "Like collecting bugs." That seemed appropriate.

We were nearing Saturn again. Just the sight of those beautiful rings, sparkling, twinkling good-bye; I almost cried.

The deep blackness with occasional zips of light was taking my mind off leaving - and off my disappearing friend. It was incredible to think we were actually sailing through space! Jupiter was coming into view and the Martians were sling-shooting past the gas giant. We seemed to be on course for home but I couldn't shake the feeling that something was not quite right, that something was about to happen.

And something did. Slowly, creepily, an object, a being was materialising from the surrounding air. It wasn't our Robotron since he was beside us and beginning to beep loudly. Oh no! Not you-know-who again!

We should have listened to Robbie - he was obviously warning us. And the thing he was warning us about was a really, truly fearsome alien! Rapella had taken on a new look: horns, spiky head, slitty eyes, slimy skin. It didn't suit her.

She was advancing on us as if there was something she wanted. Or was she trying to stop us from going home? Well, I wasn't putting up with that! I yanked the Robotron's controls from out of Max's hand - I was that angry!

Quickly I programmed Robbie to "contain" Rapella. A high-pitched scream erupted from the alien. "Don't hurt me!" it called out in Pella's voice. "I am afraid!"

I hesitated. I didn't know what to do. After all, this alien used to be my best friend. I pressed "Cancel" on the Robotron's control. Max looked at me as if I'd suddenly turned stupid.

"Don't listen to her! Attack, Robbie, attack!" he shouted, trying to get the control away from me.

Robbie did as he was told. He was not only a voice-activated robot but obviously more interested in taking orders from a boy than a girl.

The Robotron's arms emerged in quick succession - he seemed to be manufacturing them himself!

He wove in and out, pushing, shoving, producing more and more arms - almost flying!

Rapella was attempting to fight back - and she was fast! And fierce! But Robbie was faster - and becoming quite fierce! He wrapped several arms and several ropes around her horns, head, limbs. With one last twang he folded her into a neat, tidy package.

Sighs of relief filled the module. Ejecting the bundle, that was once my best friend, into outer space did not fill me with the joy it should have. In fact, I felt a bit sad for the friendship, however brief, we had once had. But she - it - was gone, out into the vastness of the Universe.

Moog sensed how bad I was feeling and offered me a green algae shake. It didn't help.

"What sort of algae is it?" I whispered to Max who was also slurping one.

"Spiralina," he whispered back. "Two hundred times more protein than beef."

Nice name. Shame about the yuk factor.

Chapter 12 - The Journey Home

The journey back proved just as eventful as the journey to Saturn. There were a few near misses with a couple of comets but luckily Zoog was able to pass through the tails. The Martian ship zipped around the meteorites we encountered and luckily we didn't have to send the Robotron out again to repair any damage.

But Robbie had had enough of Max and I bossing him around; he spent the rest of the trip playing computer games with Caracatus and Iota. Humphrey and Alpha were floating through the corridors, chasing each other and doing somersaults.

Max couldn't help wondering how to explain this trip once we got home. Then he decided it was probably best not to try.

However, we weren't there yet. The asteroid where we had met the Martians was no longer in place - it had moved on. Without an anchor to attach our cable we weren't going to get back to the Space Station or the submarine base - or home.

The Martians looked confident, as they always did, and assured us they would return us to Earth.

Oogli Woogli shook his tentacles at Max and I and waved us over. "Would you not like to come back to

Mars? We could play Astroball and explore the Universe. And beyond."

Tempting as that sounded - and I knew Max was tempted - I wanted to go back to our blue-green planet. There was a time for exploring the Universe and a time for going home - and I knew which one I wanted.

Max and Oogli Woogli were still talking, reminiscing about our visit to Mars, while I went in search of the Professor.

"What's happening?" I asked.

"Well," began the Professor, sideburns twitching, "our friends want to take us closer so we can transfer to the Space Station."

"Won't that be risky for them? I mean, how are we going to explain a Martian spaceship dropping us off?"

The Professor nodded. "But they have been working on an invisibility cloak."

"An invisibility cloak?" Had we been up in space too long? "Making the ship invisible - or us?" I asked.

"Us. It means disassembling and then re-assembling our atoms."

"Really? In the same order, I hope."

The Professor had obviously been thinking the same thing. "Well, we've got to trust them. They haven't let us down yet."

True, but when it came to my atoms, I didn't want anyone - including Martians - messing with them.

We were getting closer to the Space Station. We said goodbye to Oog, Zoog, Moog and Oogli Woogli and promised to keep in touch. Max told Caracatus he would miss him. I tried not to cry.

Instructions were given. Entering a tube was the easy part - being disassembled wasn't. But in a split second we were "zapped" onto the Space Station, re-assembled - in the same order. Then Max and I fell asleep, which was just as well. It made it easier for the Professor and Robbie to pack us, Alpha and Humphrey up. We zipped back down the space elevator to the base station where the ferry was waiting.

And then the problems began.

We'd had a pretty good trip up till then but as Professor Boggle brought us into Max's house, his mother ran towards him.

She hugged him hard and demanded to know, "Max, where have you been? Are you alright? We couldn't get in touch with you! Nobody seems to have heard of this Science Camp!" She gave the Professor an angry look. "And Milky's parents are beside themselves with worry. They haven't heard from you either, dear." I wasn't saying anything.

Max's mother turned to the Professor. "Uncle Septimus, I'm ashamed of you! You've been gone three months. You were supposed to be getting Max into another school - you promised!"

Professor Boggle tried to look ashamed but wasn't doing a good job of it. Max tried not to look pleased that

88

he had missed school. But then he'd learnt a lot while we'd been away, as had I.

"But where have you been?" his mother continued. "Off on one of your adventures, I suppose? For all I know you were all floating around in outer space!"

Max and the Professor looked at each other and tried not to smile. I was still keeping quiet.

His father came into the kitchen. "Never again, Max. Do you hear me? You've upset your mother terribly. You are never to go to the Professor's house again. And that's final."

"Yes, Dad."

"And Milky will stay with us until her parents return."

"Yes, Dad."

"Never ever again," his father repeated.

"I'd better go," said Professor Boggle. "Will you see me out? Max, Milky?"

We went outside and closed the door. The animals were obediently waiting for us.

The Professor explained to Humphrey that Alpha would be coming to live with them. Pella, or Rapella, had used the little dog in order to appear more human - all humans liked dogs. Now Alpha had nowhere else to go.

I could tell Humphrey was getting ready for a growl and a grumble. But then he just gave what I guessed was a cat shrug. We said goodbye to Humphrey and Alpha. He grunted, she licked our faces.

Max and I hugged Professor Boggle, said how much we had enjoyed this adventure, how much we had learnt. And how much we would miss him. We tried not to cry.

"Goodbye Milky, goodbye Max," the Professor said loudly. "Take good care of yourselves."

Then he bent down and whispered, "Never say 'never'. Or 'ever'. Or 'never ever again'."

And he winked, waved and boggled off.